This Walker book belongs to:

_____

_____

_____

First published 1999 by Walker Books Ltd
87 Vauxhall Walk, London SE11 5HJ

This edition published 2016

2 4 6 8 10 9 7 5 3 1

Text © 1999 Sarah Wilson
Illustrations © 1999 Melissa Sweet

This book has been typeset in Lemonade

Printed in China

British Library Cataloguing in Publication Data:
a catalogue record for this book is available from the British Library

ISBN 978-1-4063-7112-3

www.walker.co.uk

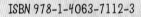

Love and Kisses

Sarah Wilson

illustrated by
Melissa Sweet

WALKER BOOKS
AND SUBSIDIARIES
LONDON · BOSTON · SYDNEY · AUCKLAND

Blow a kiss and let it go.

You never know how love will grow –

Smooch
and smack!
You kiss your cat.

Your cat may kiss a cow.

The cow may kiss a giggling goose,

The goose, a fish – somehow!

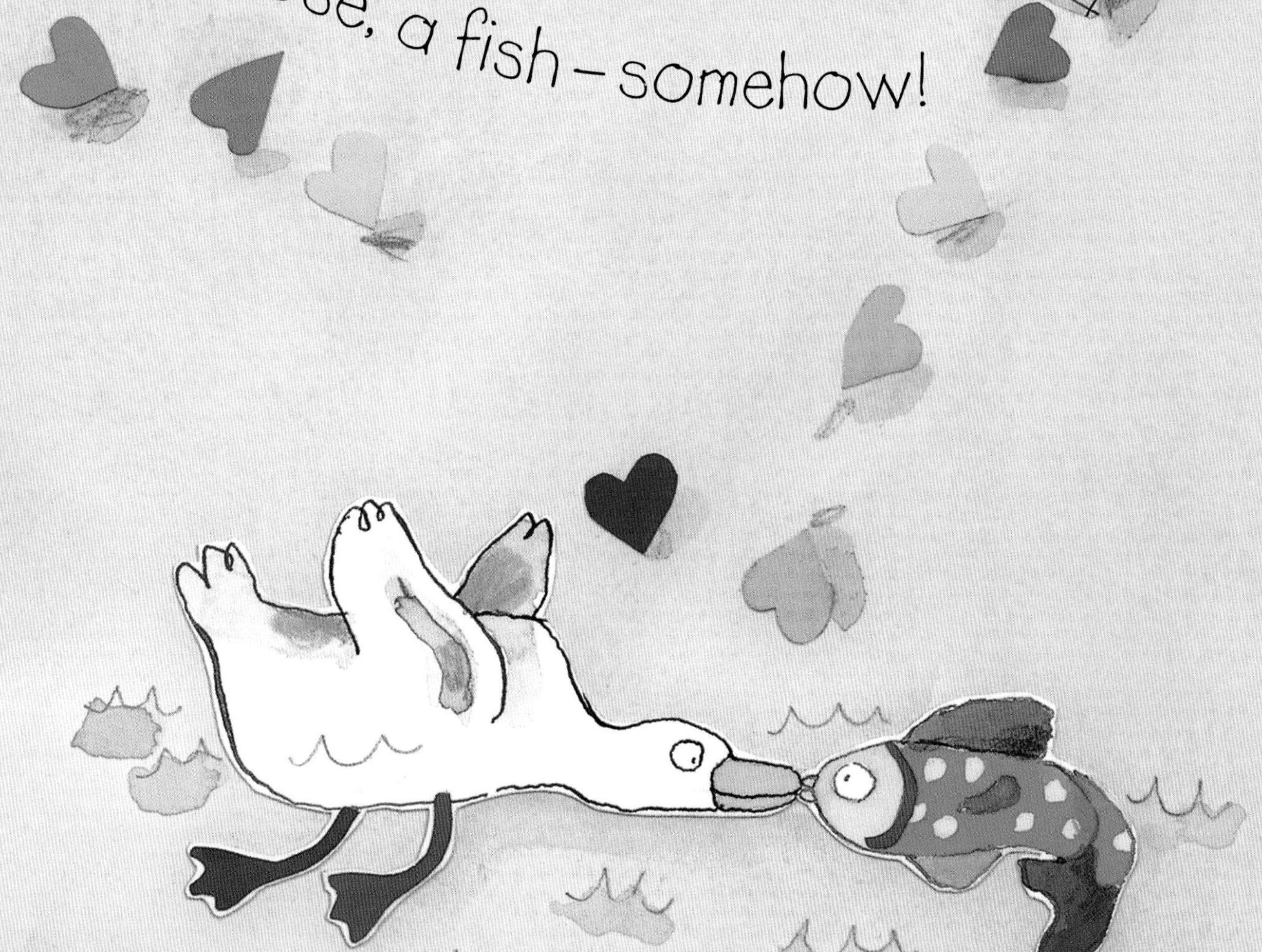

The fish—
splish!
splash!—may kiss a fox.

The fox may kiss a frog.

The frog may jump to plant a kiss

upon a friendly dog.

The dog may kiss a frisky horse

and catch him by surprise!

The horse may kiss a red-winged bird

with twinkles in her eyes.

The bird may fly to kiss a cow,
who'll laugh a great big

The cow may run to kiss a cat,

who'll then kiss ...

you-know-who!

Kisses! Kisses!

Smooch and SMACK!

- you'll have your love
and kisses back!